To little puddle splashers everywhere,
especially: Bridgett, Dryden, Callaghan,
Archer, Jett, and Zion. —S.M.

For Anne, David, and Jessica.
My anchor, my life, my light. —C.W.

Welcome, Rain!

BY **Sheryl McFarlane**

ILLUSTRATED BY
Christine Wei

GREYSTONE KIDS

GREYSTONE BOOKS • VANCOUVER/BERKELEY/LONDON

Good morning, Rain.
I like your fresh happy smell,
and the robins and chickadees
gobbling tasty earthworm treats
like you too.

Let's play, Rain.
I'm jumping, laughing, skipping,
splashing in your muddy puddles
with my yellow rubber boots
and my little brother.

I'm glad you're here, Rain.
The strawberries need you,
and the pea and carrot seeds
I helped Gran plant
need you too.

Thank you, Rain,

for the water from our taps

to cook spaghetti and wash up after.

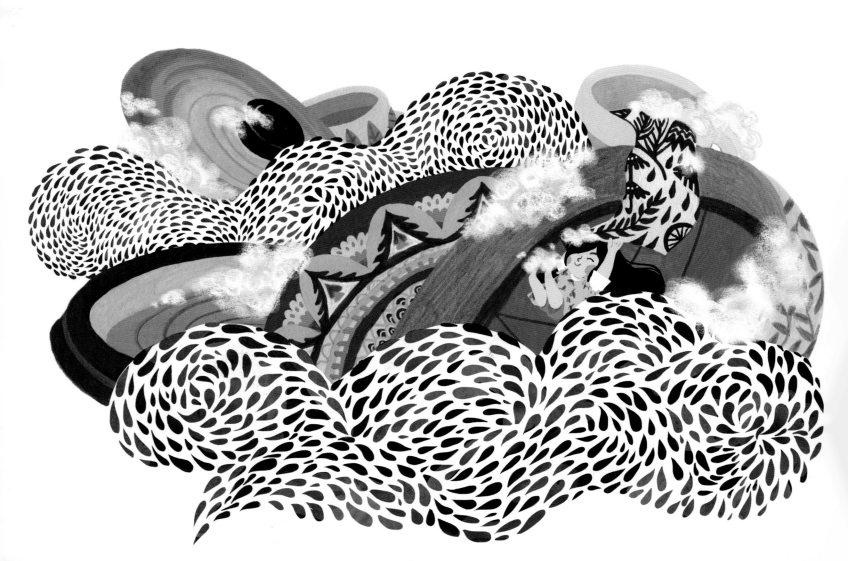

Thank you for the water for my bath
and for Mom's herbal tea.

But maybe that's enough now, Rain.
The creeks and lakes are full
and the birds are huddled in our trees,
fluffing up their feathers
so they can stay warm and dry.

Not now, Rain.

I don't want you and your thunder friends
to scare my little dog, Ruby.
I hug her close so she knows
that she is safe.

Goodbye, Rain.

Goodbye, rain suits and rubber boots.

I am lightning fast

on my scooter,

but I wait at the corner

for my mom and my little brother.

Don't worry about us, Rain.

We have Gran's sprinkler to run through

and a wading pool
on hot days.

We have sugar snap peas and watermelon
and Gran's strawberry shortcake.

But don't stay gone forever, Rain.
It's too hot for sidewalk chalk
or catching frogs with my little brother,

and it's way too sweaty
at night to sleep.

We miss you, Rain.
The grass is brown
and too itchy to play on,
and the trees and flowers
that drink you up
miss you more than we do.

Welcome, Rain!

So glad you're back, Rain.
I like catching your drops on my tongue
and the way you sparkle on spiderwebs.
I like dancing in your rainbow showers
with my friends.

We need you, Rain.
You keep the forest green and growing
for beetles, bears, and cougars,
and you fill the lakes and streams
for ducks, frogs, and fish.

Good night, Rain.
You are a bedtime pitter-patter lullaby
playing on the roof.
You are a drip-drop song of raindrops
singing in the trees.

Still, I wonder, Rain . . .

now that the leaves are gone

and it's getting cold . . .

would you please,

could you please,

come again as snow?

Greystone Kids / Greystone Books Ltd.
greystonebooks.com

Cataloguing data available from Library and Archives Canada
ISBN 978-1-77164-695-6 (cloth)
ISBN 978-1-77164-696-3 (epub)

Editing by Kallie George
Copy editing by Elizabeth McLean
Proofreading by Doeun Rivendell
Jacket and text design by Sara Gillingham Studio
The illustrations in this book were rendered in mixed media.

Printed and bound in Malaysia on FSC® certified paper by Papercraft.
The FSC® label means that materials used for the product have been responsibly sourced.

Greystone Books thanks the Canada Council for the Arts, the British Columbia Arts
Council, the Province of British Columbia through the Book Publishing Tax Credit,
and the Government of Canada for supporting our publishing activities.

Canadä

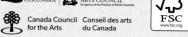

Greystone Books gratefully acknowledges the xʷməθkʷəy̓əm (Musqueam),
Sḵwx̱wú7mesh (Squamish), and səl̓ilwətaɬ (Tsleil-Waututh) peoples on
whose land our Vancouver head office is located.